Pageturners Ltd.
35 Cambridge Road, Hove
www.devoted-ebooks.com

First Edition September 2015

ISBN-13: 978-1517490904
ISBN-10: 1517490901

Printed in the United Kingdom

Chapter One

In Charlie's experience most thefts were straightforward. A pickpocket, a robbery. Luggage snatched from a stagecoach. But this crime was different. The murder made no sense.

He eyed the corpse, outstretched on the wooden floorboards. The long hair was matted with blood and her face was battered beyond all recognition. Glimpses of her hands and legs under the white nightshirt showed her to have been young.

'If you can find the silver thimble,' the man was saying, 'you'll find our maid's murderer and prove my wife innocent.'

'This is where your maid slept?' Charlie asked, taking in the attic. He was trying to put his finger on what was wrong with the scene. His eyes flicked to the window. Charlie rarely passed beyond London's thick protective wall and out onto the yokel mud-tracks beyond Ald Gate.

Down on the street, Brick Lane workers were pressing clay, hauling bricks. A milkmaid with a black eye led a skinny cow door-to-door. Plain-dressed goodwives were going about their business. Two men were manhandling a reluctant ram to Bethnal Green.

The man nodded. Fitzgilbert. His name floated back to Charlie through the haze of death. He had the beet-red nostrils and watery blue eyes of a habitual snuff-taker. There was something familiar about his ratty features that Charlie couldn't yet place.

'Her room was grand for a maid,' observed Charlie, taking in the scattering of plain furnishings. There was a table, chair and a rug, moth-eaten to shreds. Many families of ten didn't own as much.

A piece of broken mirror had been set into the eaves. Charlie saw his own expressive brown eyes reflected back, narrowed in thought.

Framed in the glass he could see a thick cluster of wooden crosses arranged by the window. His eyes switched to the chimney breast, where Bible passages had been chalked in a careful hand. Dust had been disturbed in the hearth, he noticed.

He had that uneasy feeling again. There was more to the room than met the eye. He glanced at the desecrated face. The attack could have been a robbery, he supposed. Certainly there were violent villains in this part of London. He moved forward. The injuries to the face seemed more … personal. As though someone had taken pains to etch out this poor girl.

'We meant to have more servants here,' Fitzgilbert was saying. 'But my wife's condition … And now people say she murdered poor Nancy …'

His voice cracked. Charlie put a hand on Fitzgilbert's shoulder and saw his reflected self do the same. They made a strange pair – Fitzgilbert's close-cropped hair and spotless white collar next to Charlie's battered old gentleman's coat and unkempt dark-blond hair. With the exception of Charlie's bare feet, they looked like a Roundhead and a Cavalier from twenty years ago. As an orphan growing up in London Charlie had never got on with shoes.

'They say you're the best,' Fitzgilbert went on, taking a shuddering breath. 'The best thief-taker in London. Whoever killed our maid stole that silver thimble. If you find it, you catch the killer. I'm certain of it.'

Fitzgilbert brought out a snuff box, flicked a precise quantity onto his thumb and took a heavy sniff. He squinted, sneezed three times in fast succession, then inhaled a second dose.

Charlie's eyes settled back on the disused fireplace. He moved towards the chimney. A little flurry of footprints patterned the dusty boards.

'Everyone loved Nancy,' Fitzgilbert said, wiping his nose with a plain handkerchief. 'This was a terrible crime.'

'Maybe someone loved her too much,' said Charlie, stepping inside the hearth. 'It's a better reason to murder a girl than a thimble. Did she use the fire recently?' he added.

'Nancy hasn't lit that fire since winter,' said Fitzgilbert. 'She was from Lancashire. Didn't feel the cold.'

Charlie took a tinderbox from deep in his buttoned coat and sparked the flint. The flare of light was enough. There was something hidden here. Pushed tight into the side of the brick chimney.

He reached up and grasped hold. Dust and soot drifted downwards as he worked it free.

An old shoe had been hidden high in the chimney.

'This was put here recently,' observed Charlie. 'It's not been damaged by fire or smoke.'

Fitzgilbert was staring. They both knew what this meant. It was a common practice to place shoes in the chimneys of haunted houses.

'Someone put this here to ward off evil,' said Charlie. 'Your wife?'

'Elizabeth is extremely devout,' said Fitzgilbert. 'My wife doesn't believe in charms and talismans. She won't even dance a Maypole.'

'Did anyone else come up to this attic?'

'Only Nancy. It must have been she who placed it,' conceded Fitzgilbert. He was looking at the shoe as though it were cursed. 'But she never said anything to us,' he added, 'about fear of a haunting.'

Charlie examined the shoe. It was old and worn. A woman's, but much too expensive for a maid.

The strangeness of the attic room was making sense now. Charlie's eyes went to the little forest of crosses arranged by the window, the careful Bible script chalked on the walls.

She wasn't devout. She was scared.

'So your maid was frightened of something,' he said, turning the shoe. 'Or someone.'

Chapter Two

'I've never seen it before,' insisted Fitzgilbert as he led Charlie back down the stairs and through the large house. Each room they passed was bizarrely plain. There were no wall hangings, no paintings, no rugs. Just a huge cross and a Bible in every room. It was more like a monastery than a home.

It's like Cromwell's still alive, thought Charlie, remembering the monochrome London in the years after the civil war.

'You're certain you don't recognise the shoe?' pressed Charlie.

'It's not a style Elizabeth would wear,' said Fitzgilbert firmly. 'She favours sober dress. Plain black shoes. Buckles. This is … It's a frivolous kind of thing.' He looked warily at the shoe.

They walked through the Fitzgilberts' unadorned front door and Charlie felt Brick Lane's clay soil between his bare toes.

Up ahead women squatted, cutting at vast mounds of red earth with string to extract stones. Men slapped loaves of clay into moulds. The wide road east was paved with drying bricks and tiles like the scales of a great sleeping dragon.

'A single old shoe to ward off witches and bad things,' said Charlie, plumbing his memory. It was a common enough charm for Londoners, if they suspected an evil spirit.

He weighed it in his hand. The curved little heel, the embroidered sides. Whoever it fitted might have answers. He opened the buttoned front to see if the toe-prints inside gave any clue. Within was a poorly woven corn dolly.

'She was frightened of demons?' he asked, examining the poppet. It was a rough approximation of a man with a stubbly beard. A crude cross had been strapped to the figure.

Fitzgilbert stared at the shoe. His hand went reflexively to his own neatly bearded face.

Behind them shouts went up. The workers were getting ready to light the kiln. Trays of bricks were ferried past in earnest. One of the brickmakers nodded his head in mock salute to Fitzgilbert.

'Lord Sneezalot,' he grinned, 'let's hope your father finds you a better wife this time.'

Fitzgilbert frowned and muttered something inaudible while fumbling for his snuff box.

Charlie put the facts together.

Fitz. Illegitimate son of Gilbert.

He'd thought Fitzgilbert looked familiar. The man carried the shame of illegitimacy on his scrawny shoulders, along with the same wiry black hair and ratty features as his philandering father. This explained why he owned an expensive half-timbered house yet wore plain, pin-neat Puritan clothes. And why he could afford a costly snuff habit. The Gilberts had interests in tobacco colonies and would find money to keep scandal at bay. Fitzgilbert's case had suddenly become more interesting.

'I never … Nancy never said anything about demons.' Fitzgilbert was looking distractedly at the departing brickmaker. He worked snuff into his nostril.

Charlie turned the poppet in his hands.

A good Christian girl and an attic full of heathen charms.

'How came your maid to have silver?' he asked.

'I don't know. The vicar told us about it,' Fitzgilbert replied, his red nose quivering. 'He saw Nancy with it in church and was concerned she might have stolen it.'

'Might she?'

Fitzgilbert shook his head violently then sneezed. 'Such a thing is impossible,' he said. 'Nancy was a good sweet Christian girl …' The words caught in his throat.

'A jealous lover?' suggested Charlie.

'Nancy had no interest in men,' said Fitzgilbert. She had none of that silliness you find in many girls.'

'Anyone else who might wish her harm?'

Another shake of the head. Fitzgilbert began dosing out more snuff.

'What of Nancy's vicar?' Charlie asked. 'Where might I find him?'

'I have no idea,' said Fitzgilbert testily. 'Nancy worshipped in some secret commoners' church. She once joked it should be Baptist, not Puritan, for all the damp inside. Our faith are sadly persecuted in London,' he added bitterly. 'My wife and I are forced to worship privately in my father's chapel.'

Charlie brought the picture of the girl's corpse to mind. The features had been caved in, the frenzy of blows making it hard to discern a weapon shape. But at the sides of the face, the injuries were straight-edged and palm-width. Something with a flat heavy base like a candlestick, Charlie thought.

'Why was your wife accused?' he asked, watching Fitzgilbert carefully. In his experience, young maidservants and old masters went hand in hand with trouble.

Fitzgilbert glanced nervously at the brickmakers. Several women had stood to watch their conversation. He raised his snuff-loaded thumb and inhaled the entire quantity. Charlie winced.

'My wife speaks in tongues, Mr Tuesday,' Fitzgilbert said, working his nostril to keep the snuff inside. 'It's a noble condition, well known in ancient, kinder times.' He shook his head disgustedly, looking to the leather-aproned men loading kiln bricks.
'The people here don't understand,' he said, lowering his voice.
'They accuse her of terrible things.' He made a succession of near-sneezes. 'They call her *witch*.'

Chapter Three

Fitzgilbert was pointing up at the attic window.

From this angle his house looked outsized and looming next to the small wooden dwellings near to Bethnal Green's grassy expanse.

'It must have been through the window,' confirmed Fitzgilbert. 'He got in that way. The front door hadn't been broken open. Neither had the downstairs windows. But Nancy's attic window was open. She never would have left it so.'

The window casement was small, Charlie thought, for a robber burly enough to inflict such damage on a victim. He glanced along the muddy road. Corn dollies were strung in doorways. Livestock grazed. Rib-thin vagrants dozed under hedges. Over everything was the roar of the kiln, the shouts of the men and the red dust of the brickworks.

'You believe a robber learned of Nancy's silver thimble, broke in and stole it?' Charlie surmised, looking at the tiny casement.

'An apprentice saw from the street, Nancy's blood spattered on the attic window.' Fitzgilbert pointed at the diamond-paned glass, which was flecked with dried blood. 'The boy started raving. We heard him from our bed chamber. A tanner or brick boy by his clothes. Horrid creature he was. Great mop of lice-ridden ginger hair,' Fitzgilbert mimed. 'Loud gutter-London accent.' His face puckered at the memory. 'He was shouting of my wife's witchcraft. A mob gathered. They insisted on seeing inside the room. That was how we found Nancy.'

'And they took your wife?'

'Dragged her from her bed and took her straight to the Clink prison,' said Fitzgilbert. The full horror of this seemed to be dawning on him. He buried his ratty features in his hands. 'She languishes with felons!' he cried.

Fitzgilbert's eyes had misted slightly. His trembling hands reached for the snuff box. 'My poor wife. With age, she is less certain. Confused of things. But she is a gentle Christian soul who would never … Certainly, she couldn't have done that.'

Fitzgilbert was blinking rapidly, his eyes flicking to the attic window. 'She couldn't have done that,' he repeated in a whisper.

He seemed to be convincing himself. So will you help?' he asked. 'I can pay well. But I must ask for discretion and speed. This must be resolved quickly for the sake of my family name.'

He tipped snuff, sniffed, sneezed.

Charlie hesitated.

'I can only undertake to find the thimble,' he said, meeting Fitzgilbert's pale blue eyes. 'I'm a thief-taker. I have no authority to find a murderer.'

'Find the thimble and you'll find the killer,' said Fitzgilbert firmly.

'If that's the outcome, I'll be sure the criminal is brought to justice,' said Charlie carefully.

He was thinking of the tiny attic window, high up and hard to enter. From what he'd seen, the girl's murder was an inside job.

'But if I find the thimble,' continued Charlie, 'and it isn't in the killer's possession, you must still pay my dues.'

Fitzgilbert nodded, but he was thinking. Charlie put out his hand quickly, before the other man could piece together the subtext.

If your wife isn't innocent, I don't want you to renege on payment.

Fitzgilbert shook Charlie's hand automatically.

'I'll make haste,' promised Charlie. 'I know who buys and sells silver in the City. I'll ask some questions, find some answers.'

Fitzgilbert looked relieved. 'The sooner the villain is caught the better,' he said.

Charlie nodded in reply. But he didn't add what he was really thinking.

There's a good chance she's already behind bars.

Chapter Four

The Bucket of Blood tavern was Charlie's favourite place in London. The half-timbered interior was warmed by a range fire and a steaming cauldron of meat puddings. Casks of good ale lined the broad central table, and barefoot boys milled among the cheerful drinkers, selling cakes and provisions. You didn't want for anything in the Bucket if you had money or friends. And it was the best place in the City for information.

'The silver thimble hasn't been sold,' said the silversmith, shaking his head and taking a long swig of ale.

'You're certain?' said Charlie, raising his voice over the din. The tavern was hosting a prizefight, and bare-knuckled boxers were slugging it out in the corner.

'Not to anyone who deals in silver,' said the silversmith. 'That thimble hasn't changed hands in London.' He shook his grizzled head again. A little bear of a man, he wore a thick cambric doublet and matching blue breeches. Around his neck hung a medley of grimed silver wares: spoons, rings and snuff boxes.

'The thimble might already have been sold at a market,' suggested Charlie. 'Or somewhere outside the City.'

The silversmith shrugged.

'It's possible. But the thief would have got a common metal price for it,' he said. 'Barely worth the risk of hanging.'

Charlie thought back to the crime. Nothing suggested an opportunist or stupid thief.

'Melted down?' he suggested. 'Fashioned into something else?'

The silversmith shook his head with certainty.

'Not a drop of silver gets melted without the Guild's say-so. You'd need a furnace such as we have. I'd know if a thimble had been cast in its great red belly.'

The silversmith, Charlie remembered, was prone to a poetic turn of phrase when drinking. Soon after came the singing. Charlie's gaze lighted on a boy with a tray of pies.

'Something to eat?' he suggested, turning the few pennies in his pocket. It was important to keep the man sober.

'I'd rather keep room for the beer,' replied the silversmith genially, taking another deep swig.

There was a shout from the crowd. One of the boxers had landed a particularly impressive blow. Blood splattered the sawdust.

The silversmith winced. 'Who did you bet on?' he asked, eyeing the burly fighters.

'The winner,' replied Charlie, taking a long sip of beer. 'Why would a maid own a silver thimble?' he said, thinking out loud.

'It was the fashion during Cromwell's time to have them instead of engagement rings,' said the silversmith. 'Some Puritan folk keep the tradition.' He leaned back to observe the fight. 'They won't have jewels or trinkets or useless things.'

'I didn't know that,' said Charlie, wondering if Fitzgilbert had.

'The betrothed girl gets a thimble,' explained the silversmith. 'She uses it to sew her dowry clothes.' He grinned, revealing a silver denture plate welded with dead men's teeth. 'No one can accuse the bride-to-be of frivolity, for her betrothal gift was put to good use,' he concluded.

'So Nancy, the good Christian girl was secretly betrothed,' said Charlie thoughtfully.

One of the fighters hit the floor with a crash. Cheers went up. The fallen man staggered up, pulled over a table and righted himself to riotous shouts.

'Do they have any particular features, these betrothal thimbles?' asked Charlie.

The silversmith considered. 'Nothing I can call to mind,' he said eventually. 'Puritans aren't for fancy decorations. Perhaps a little more working. A turned edge, more patterning. They cannot make them too elaborate, you see. For fear of upsetting God.'

He crossed himself.

'But then the girl has two gifts instead of one,' Charlie pointed out. 'They must have a band for the ceremony.'

'Women are clever, are they not?' grinned the silversmith. 'Especially when it comes to weddings.' He nudged Charlie. 'You'd know about that,' he added.

Charlie, infamous for choosing the wrong women, gave a slight smile.

'A good thing too,' opined the silversmith. 'Cromwell's republic nearly starved us jewel men. Plain dress and nothing showy.' He shook his head. 'You'll never hear me say a bad word against King Charles,' he concluded, lifting his tankard. 'His mistresses have been the making of me.'

'There can't be many betrothal thimbles made now,' said Charlie. 'Can you find out who made one recently?'

The silversmith looked meaningfully at his empty tankard.

Charlie refilled it and chalked a mark by his symbol on the barrel. He flicked a glance at the two fighters. They were rounding on one another warily, panting with exhaustion. Charlie was relying on the outcome to settle his tab.

'It's not a common item nowadays,' agreed the silversmith, as Charlie handed him the foaming beer. 'I might be able to find out who commissioned it. But not if it were struck during Cromwell's rule,' he added. 'Too many thimbles. Too long ago.'

'How long would it take you to find out?'

The silversmith drained half the tankard in one.

'Give me a day or so,' he said. 'I'll ask about. Only three men who do that kind of work. If I learn something, I'll find you.' He tipped the last few drops from the tankard into his mouth, nodded thanks and left the Bucket of Blood.

While Charlie was thinking over his next move, the bare-knuckle match ended and the bloodied victor pocketed his prize money. Charlie raised a hand and beckoned him. The boxer grinned a gap-toothed smile and sauntered over.

'A good fight, John,' said Charlie, slapping him on the back. 'You must have enough to marry that girl of yours by now.'

'Next week,' said John, grinning. 'We're in your debt. I'd still be hod-carrying for fourpence if you hadn't arranged my first fight. What brings you to the Bucket?'

'I'm in search of a silver thimble,' said Charlie. 'Stolen from a murdered Puritan girl.'

'A murdered Puritan,' said John, wrinkling his nose. 'Them black and white folks?'

'Cromwell's religion,' agreed Charlie. 'From before our Merry Monarch.' He eyed John's bulky physique. 'Would you like to repay that favour?' he asked.

'Any time you ask it of me,' replied the boxer genially. His face was flush with drink and victory.

'How about now?' said Charlie. 'I need muscle. We're going to the Clink.'

Chapter Five

The guard led them down the steps into the Clink. Charlie steadied his breathing. He had a deep dislike of prisons and a healthy distrust of gaolers. Having grown up an orphan in the City, he had always obeyed the cardinal rule of those who danced in the twilight of legality.

Never enter a prison without a friend larger than the gaoler.

While John plodded next to him through the narrow corridors, whistling the cheerful tune of a law-abiding man, Charlie's litany of goods-off-the-back-of-carts, angry husbands and starving thieves he'd let escape the noose rolled through his mind.

The damp corridors closed tighter around them and the air grew impossibly humid and stinking. They passed a furnace where manacles and a selection of hideous tools were laid ready for use. A low babble of moans washed over them.

'Mistress Fitzgilbert is one of the lucky ones,' opined the gaoler as they approached several thick doors. 'Her husband paid for a private cell.'

'Has she had any visitors?' asked Charlie.

'You're the first. People fear gaol fever. It's rife.'

As he spoke, eyes began appearing at the narrow gratings of the cells. Charlie heard a reedy voice beg for bread. The guard thumped a door and the sound ceased.

'Doesn't do to keep them well fed,' said the turnkey philosophically. 'Gives 'em ideas. This way,' he added. 'She's the door at the end.'

Charlie slipped behind John, and pushed a piece of bread he'd stowed for his dinner through the cell grating. He heard hands fall on it hungrily.

Now the gaoler was unlocking Elizabeth Fitzgilbert's cell with a large key.

Charlie couldn't say what he'd been expecting to see. A mad woman cowed with fear perhaps, or staring out at them in confusion. But he wasn't at all prepared for the calm countenance that greeted them.

Elizabeth Fitzgilbert was in her early forties, sitting tall and erect with straight handsome features and large green eyes. Her brown hair was mostly hidden beneath an old-fashioned cloth cap and she wore a sober black dress with a large white collar. A plain brass cross hung around her neck and a small Bible was her only noticeable possession.

She looked like a woman who had not been told Cromwell had died and a flamboyant king now sat on the throne.

Elizabeth stood to greet them. Charlie watched her buckled black shoes scrape the muddied straw.

'The Thief-Taker,' she said, bobbing a half-curtsy. 'My husband wrote, telling me to expect you.'

'What did he tell you to expect?' asked Charlie, thrown by her calm manner.

'He said you would prove my innocence,' she said. Her large eyes suggested she wasn't sure of this herself. 'He seems to have great faith in you.'

Her eyes landed on John.

'Perhaps you have means I'm unfamiliar with,' she added, looking now at Charlie's scarred face.

'Incident with a horse,' said Charlie, touching the kink in his nose and the sliver of scar on his lip. He winked. 'I tell larger men it was a knife fight.'

Elizabeth gave a brief smile.

'But I'm not here to prove your innocence,' he added. 'I'm a thief-taker. Here to find the silver thimble.' He paused. Elizabeth's eyes had darkened.

'You're not a good man as I hoped,' she muttered.

'No,' agreed Charlie apologetically. 'Your husband …' he added, 'you're not what I expected.'

She lifted an eyebrow.

'You expected someone confused? Raving? My husband does like to exaggerate my condition,' she said.

'What is your condition?'

'I can't say for certain,' said Elizabeth. 'Only sometimes I wake up and don't know what happened. My husband tells me I rave. Speak in tongues. It doesn't happen often. But it makes me seem devout, you see. Touched by angels. And my husband is very concerned that we are seen as proper.'

'His illegitimacy?' guessed Charlie. 'He's ashamed of it?'

'All bastards are,' said Elizabeth. 'And with Lord Gilbert's drinking and carousing, my poor husband has a heavy atonement to bear. But you didn't come here to talk of his religious fervour.'

'No.' Charlie drew out the shoe. 'I came to talk of this.'

Something seemed to shrink back in Elizabeth's eyes.

'What would I know of that?' she said.

'I would expect a great deal,' said Charlie. 'Since this is your shoe.'

Chapter Six

Elizabeth sat straight-backed, her face impassive.

'What makes you say that?' she said.

You just told me, thought Charlie.

'I've an eye for detail,' he said aloud, holding out the shoe. Charlie nodded to the muddy footprints on the gaol floor. 'It looks the right size for your foot,' he added, placing the shoe next to an identically sized print.

'You can't be certain of that.'

'Put it on and prove me wrong,' he said.

Elizabeth hesitated. Then she sighed.

'It's from before my marriage. Puritans are scathing of frivolous things. But some belongings … Some things I kept. A dress. A few gloves and shoes. My husband doesn't know,' she added, glancing up at Charlie.

'Did you give the shoe to Nancy?'

Elizabeth nodded. 'She needed an old shoe,' she said. 'For some charm or other.'

'She didn't say what the charm was for?'

'Protection, or good luck or some such.' Elizabeth shrugged. 'She was a country girl. From Lancashire. Nancy had some strange ways, but they kept her happy. So long as she went to church we didn't begrudge it.'

There was something in Elizabeth's face that didn't quite fit what she was saying.

'What other strange ways did she have?' asked Charlie, watching her carefully.

Elizabeth smiled faintly. 'Nothing different from most country maids. There was a fortune-teller she went to see after church on Sundays. Old Joan or Jenny or the like.'

'Do you know where this fortune-teller practised?'

Charlie recalled Fitzgilbert's description of Nancy. The sensible girl who only left the house to visit church.

'Somewhere near Ald Gate. She never mentioned the street.'

Charlie sucked at his scarred lip in frustration. The streets around Ald Gate were clustered with fortune-tellers conning silly women from their pennies.

'Your husband thinks Nancy only left the house for church,' he said.

That faint smile again. 'My husband was mistaken, Mr Thief-Taker. But men tended to be, when it came to Nancy.'

'She had a way with men?' suggested Charlie.

'Her beauty was only part of it,' said Elizabeth, her eyes far away. 'Nancy was captivating. She could compel people to do whatever she wanted. Not just men.' She nodded to the shoe and shook her head. 'Men became obsessed with her.'

'Which men?'

'The red-headed boy who had me arrested.' Elizabeth smiled wryly. 'He thought himself in love with her. Why else do you think he took such an interest in Nancy's bedroom window?'

'Your husband didn't mention knowing the lad,' said Charlie. 'He took your accuser for a common apprentice who happened to be passing by.'

'My husband isn't the most astute of social observers.' Elizabeth looked away. 'The red-headed boy was always skulking near the house,' she said. 'Hoping for a glimpse of Nancy. He witnessed some of my … episodes. My fits. He thought my witchcraft was keeping Nancy away from him.' She raised her eyebrows to signal the ludicrousness of this. 'That was how Nancy was. No one held her responsible for things,' she added.

'What of your husband and Nancy?' asked Charlie.

Elizabeth flinched.

'My husband is a faithful man.'

'He didn't find Nancy beautiful?'

Elizabeth's fists clenched.

'All men found Nancy beautiful,' she said shortly. 'Likely my husband looked. He may have even imagined. But he never acted upon it.'

'How can you be so certain?' pressed Charlie.

She smiled thinly. 'He's a bastard son. Hanging by a thread on Lord Gilbert's favour. His reputation could take no misdeed.'

'What of Nancy's reputation?'

'Everyone thought her an angel,' said Elizabeth. She gave a scoffing kind of laugh and Charlie heard bitterness.

'You didn't think of her as pure?'

'No, Mr Tuesday, I did not.'

'Nancy had lovers?' he asked.

'How else would she come to possess a silver thimble?' Elizabeth gave a sad smile. 'Men see purity when it suits them. And it always seems to match a pretty face.' She lifted her eyes to Charlie's. 'I feel sorry for men in that way,' she concluded.

'What of your husband?' asked Charlie. 'Do you feel sorry for him?'

Something twitched in her face then. Fear or hurt. It was gone almost as quickly, but they both knew Charlie had seen the slip.

'You didn't marry for love,' Charlie discerned.

She let out a long sigh.

'There's nothing in the Bible to condemn it. I am a good and obedient wife to him.'

'But you've no children.'

Her green eyes flicked sharply up at Charlie.

'God never blessed us. I am a good wife, Mr Tuesday. I always did my wifely duty.'

'There is something you don't tell me,' said Charlie. 'About the thimble. I usually know when people are lying to me. But mostly it's to save their own skin. You stand accused of witchcraft and I think you know something that could prove your innocence.'

Elizabeth opened her mouth and closed it again. Her hands shook very slightly.

'If I don't find the thimble,' said Charlie, 'you'll likely burn.'

A hardness settled over Elizabeth's handsome features.

'Do you believe in God's divine wisdom, Mr Tuesday?'

The question took him by surprise.

'I believe in God,' he said. 'But He's no lover of London.'

'I offer myself to God's mercy,' said Elizabeth, folding her hands. She was locked away now. A pillar of piety.

'God may be merciful,' said Charlie, growing frustrated, 'but if I had a penny for every innocent hanged I wouldn't live on Cheapside.'

'What makes you so sure I'm hiding something?'

Charlie glanced to the door. He could see the gaoler's heavy form lumbering towards them. 'It's a gift,' he said distractedly. 'If you want to prove me wrong, swear on the Bible you've told me all you know.'

Elizabeth looked away.

There was a hammering on the other side of the cell door.

'Time to go!' shouted the turnkey. 'Your visit with the witch is over.'

Chapter Seven

'Did you notice the string around her neck?' said Charlie as he and John followed the gaoler through the winding prison.

John shook his head.

'Elizabeth keeps something concealed beneath her dress,' said Charlie.

'A crucifix,' reasoned John. 'Valuable, so she hides it from the gaoler.'

He shot a glance ahead to check they couldn't be overheard.

'Could be a crucifix,' said Charlie. 'Could be a thimble. Certainly she knows something she'd rather burn for than confess.'

'Loyalty to the husband,' suggested John.

'Or she's scared of him.' Charlie's instincts were telling him this was more likely.

They passed through a thick door and up into another dark corridor.

'Nancy only left the house to visit church and a fortune-teller,' said Charlie as the guard turned the heavy lock behind them. 'If she had a lover, she likely met him at church. But why keep the betrothal secret?'

He thought for a moment.

'First I'll find Nancy's vicar,' he said. 'He saw the thimble. Maybe he can tell me something more of it. Then I'll go to Bethnal Green. Ask some questions. Try and find the red-headed apprentice.

If only we knew which fortune-teller Nancy visited. I'll wager she could tell us much.'

They were passing by longer-term felons now. Filthy arms stretched from the cell grates.

Charlie eyed John. 'I imagine your Rosie is impatient for the wedding?'

'We make each other oaths every day,' said John. 'Rosie will wash her dress especially and has made a garter from an old ribbon. She is clever in that way.' There was a far away look in his eyes. 'She is my sun and moon, Charlie,' he said. 'We shall be the happiest people you ever saw wed.'

'How should you like to buy her some extra pretty gifts for the day?'

John tilted his head, only half comprehending.

'A Puritan church won't take kindly to questions,' explained Charlie. 'Not while King Charles sends men to break them up. If you come along with me and we find the thimble, I'll be sure you're well rewarded.'

'I've never known you fail,' said John agreeably. 'I have a fight tomorrow, but can otherwise be at your disposal. My Rosie would like some coins for luck,' he added, his heavy features softening at the thought.

Charlie nodded gratefully. Infractions regularly broke out in churches. Pockets of bad feeling had festered since the civil war twenty years ago.

'First we'll have to find it,' said Charlie. 'Most Puritans worship in secret. Unless they've a private chapel like the Gilberts.'

Charlie ran through his mental map of the City.

'Nancy saw a fortune-teller near Ald Gate,' he said. 'She lived near Bethnal Green. Even Fitzgilbert wouldn't spare his maid a whole Sunday morning to say her prayers. Nancy's church must have been somewhere between the two.'

'I thought you knew all the secret places in the City,' said John.

Up ahead the gaoler slowed his pace. Something about the movement made Charlie uneasy.

'Not outside London's walls,' he said, lowering his voice. 'And Puritans keep their churches well hidden. Attics, basements.'

Charlie could sense the turnkey straining to hear their conversation.

'Nancy told Fitzgilbert her church was damp and cold,' he said, trying to dispel the fear of being locked in.

'A cellar then,' said John. 'But there's probably a hundred cellars between Bethnal Green and Ald Gate.'

'Not all are damp enough to invite comment,' said Charlie. He cast a quick look to the gaoler. 'Nancy joked her church should be Baptist for all the water.'

As he said the words something came to him. An idea.

'There's an old river that runs from Bishops Gate to Petticoat Lane,' he said, thinking aloud. 'It was covered over to stop people using it as a sewer. Plenty of water in those parts.'

Charlie pictured the houses crossing the old river near Ald Gate and Bethnal Green. There were only a handful.

They could see the door to the exit now. Charlie let out a breath he didn't know he'd been holding. He resisted the urge to run towards it.

The guard stopped and turned to them, swinging his keys thoughtfully.

'Most of the thief-takers are known to me,' he said. 'But not you.'

Charlie understood the implication. Gaolers were paid for each prisoner and more for confessions. Most thief-takers took bribes to bring in felons.

'I've an arrangement with old Noilly at Bridewell,' he lied.

The guard shook his head.

'I don't think you do,' he said. 'I've spoken to some of the other gaolers. There's a feeling Charlie Tuesday thinks himself high and mighty. Above bringing felons to the noose.'

'I get paid to return property,' replied Charlie in the same easy tone. 'What happens to the thieves isn't my concern.'

'Yet you could take a few pence more for sending them my way,' suggested the turnkey. He frowned. 'I think you know the whereabouts of a fair few guilty men.'

Charlie could see him mentally calculating his profits.

'I've a feeling you'll be staying with us a spell,' decided the gaoler. 'Just until we get a few names out of you.' His hands went to the heavy bunch of keys at his hip. Charlie glanced at the door out. It looked impossibly thick.

'I'll give you a name now,' he said, gauging the distance to the exit. 'John Smith.'

The turnkey frowned. 'Not heard of that one. What's he guilty of?'

Charlie's eyes slid across to John. He made the smallest of nods to the keys. John understood immediately.

'He's a prizefighter,' said Charlie. 'Wins every fight. Knocks men unconscious with a single blow.'

'Fighting's not a crime,' grumbled the gaoler.

'No,' said Charlie, 'but I've a feeling he'll help me escape the Clink quite soon.'

The guard's beady eyes narrowed, trying to make sense of what he'd just heard. Understanding dawned as John came at him.

The gaoler's eyes opened wide in shock as the prizefighter's massive fist crunched into his jaw, sending him spinning. Charlie darted forward and freed the bunch of keys in a quick movement. John's next punch hit the gaoler's chin, driving his head back, then a final blow drove him to the ground.

Charlie flipped the keys in his hand and raced for the door, with John behind him.

Chapter Eight

'You're losing your touch,' said Charlie, as he and John arrived on Whitechapel Lane. 'It took you three blows to land that turnkey.'

'Coulda done it in one if I'd wanted,' sniffed John. 'I prefer to save my knuckles. He was a heavy man.'

Charlie dropped to his haunches and considered the street. Immediately he felt disappointed.

'No cellars,' he said, peering along the row of neat brick and wooden houses. 'The church can't be here.' Charlie sucked his scarred lip. 'I could have sworn …'

He eyed the street again, pondering. A ditch ran alongside the houses, filled with vegetable scraps and other refuse. Somewhere beneath their feet a river ran. Charlie was certain it explained the damp in Nancy's church. But if there were no cellars, where could it be?

'Brick Lane to the east,' he muttered. 'They'll be sure to use a water source to make bricks. And there's a brewers there who need a well.'

Charlie let his mind track the direction of the hidden river. By his best reckoning it wound near to where they stood. But there was nothing here besides neat houses.

Something about that struck him as odd.

'We're a stone's throw from Brick Lane,' he said slowly. 'But these houses aren't built from new London Brick. They're made with old Roman ones.'

He pointed to the slim, worn bricks.

'So people have dug out old Roman bricks,' shrugged John. 'They do it all over London.'

'They do it near to old Roman constructions,' corrected Charlie. 'There's probably a Roman sewer nearby.'

He scanned the street. His eyes flashed as he made out a tell-tale brick arch set low in the ditch. Something had occurred to him.

'Perhaps,' said Charlie slowly, 'Fitzgilbert got it wrong. Perhaps Nancy made the Baptist joke, not because of the damp. But because of the location.'

'What do you mean?' John's large face was scrunched in puzzlement.

'There's a Roman bathhouse,' said Charlie, 'just east of Ald Gate. It floods at high tide, so lies abandoned.'

John looked at him blankly.

'Perhaps,' explained Charlie, 'Nancy was making a reference to an actual bath with her Baptist remark.' He thought for a moment. 'An old bathhouse might serve as a secret church,' he added, imagining the vaulted ceilings, the ringing acoustics. 'It's worth a look.'

Chapter Nine

The bathhouse was a decayed structure of damp Roman brick, covered over with ivy and vegetation. A mouldering entrance door, standing slightly ajar, led into darkness.

Charlie and John squeezed past the defunct door. A stench of damp greeted them. A set of stone steps, slick and green with mould, spiralled to the stone bathroom below.

'It does look awful narrow,' complained John, manoeuvring his thick bulk down the precipitous entrance behind Charlie. 'I might slip and break my neck.'

'Go slowly,' suggested Charlie, as he descended the final steps. A shaft of light from the doorway provided partial illumination.

The bathhouse was small. Damp cold stone arced into a low vaulted ceiling. The sides were lined with slab-like seating. At the centre was a walled pond of water ominously close to overflowing.

'It's cold in here,' said John, passing down the last step and eyeing the close, dark walls. 'I wouldn't like to be here when it floods,' he added, following the watermark high above their heads. 'I'll wager more than a few men have been trapped down here and met their deaths.'

Charlie's gaze moved reflexively to the high door leading out.

'We shan't be long,' he promised, surveying the interior. The regular ingress of water made it impossible to tell if anyone had been here recently. All trace had been washed away by the tides.

'It's a cistern,' said Charlie, moving closer to the small reservoir. A droplet of water fell from the ceiling and rippled across the dark depths. 'This must be where it links to the river,' he added, wondering how deep it went. 'Water rises with the tide and when it falls again, a portion is reserved in here. Clever,' he added approvingly. John didn't look sure.

Charlie moved further in, letting his eyes adjust to the dark.

'It's certainly been used as a church,' he said, taking in a large cross etched on the ceiling. 'But look at this.' He touched the damp wall. Bolts had been driven into the stone. Chains and leather cuffs hung down.

John shuddered. 'Restraints?' he whispered. 'For what?'

'They perform exorcisms here,' said Charlie, breathing out. 'I've seen this before. You bind the subject while the exorcism is carried out.'

Thoughts were rearranging themselves in his head. He was remembering the shoe with the charm inside to dispel bad spirits. Nancy's attic room.

'I think,' he said, 'Nancy may have come here to be exorcised.'

There was a sound above them. Charlie's head snapped up.

The door was closing.

He reacted instantly, racing up the slippery steps. In seconds he'd reached the head of the stair, but it was too late.

'We're trapped,' he said grimly. 'Someone wants us out of harm's way.'

Chapter Ten

The door was impenetrable. It had been blocked with something heavy.

'It's no good,' said Charlie, as John threw his huge body against it in vain. 'We can't get any weight behind it at this angle.'

'Then what?' asked John.

'It's a busy street,' said Charlie. 'If we shout for long enough—'

He was interrupted by a loud sluicing sound echoing through the bathhouse. Somewhere beneath them a waterlock had been opened.

John and Charlie exchanged glances. And then the central reservoir of water began to bubble and spill out from its confines.

John attacked the trapdoor with new vigour.

'Help!' he shouted. 'Help!'

Charlie watched helplessly as water streamed forth. Already it had covered the ring of stone seats.

'It's no good,' he told John. 'It will drown us in minutes.'

John turned in horror to see the water had now filled the small bathhouse up to the base of the steps. Water lapped at their feet.

'Where has the water come from?' he asked, open-mouthed with terror.

'The bath must connect to some old dammed waterway,' said Charlie, as water rose to their knees. 'A tributary siphoned off for other use that runs through here.'

He looked up and around, taking in their options.

'It will cover our heads soon,' he said.

'The ceiling curves,' said John. 'Perhaps there'll be a breathing space.'

'If there is we'll have to swim in it for as long as it takes to be found,' said Charlie. 'Could be days.'

He was looking at the dark cistern.

'There's another way out,' he said, pointing. 'Through there.'

John's eyes bulged with horror.

'It must go somewhere,' said Charlie reasonably. 'Otherwise the tidal water couldn't get in.'

Water had reached their waists.

'It's flowing too fast,' said Charlie. 'We need to wait until the water slows.'

'You're sure there's something on the other side?'

'I'm certain of it,' lied Charlie.

John closed his eyes. The water was at their chests.

'I'm not good underwater,' he admitted, looking into the gloomy water rising steadily. 'I'll be lost and drowned in the dark. My poor Rosie will be widowed before she is even wed.'

Charlie fumbled in his leather coat, took out a dog-eared piece of string and tied it to John's belt.

'I won't lose you,' he said, tying it to his own. 'You have my word. If we die down there, we die together.'

John nodded. But as the water reached their necks he began flailing in the water.

'We'll be drowned!' he protested. 'It comes too high!'

'It's slowing,' said Charlie with more conviction than he felt. 'A few more moments.' His heart was pounding. The current didn't seem to be easing off. Water lapped at their ears. They tipped up their heads, utilising the last of the air. Then beneath them, the swirling water seemed to slacken its pace.

'Now,' said Charlie, taking a breath. And they both plunged into the black waters.

Chapter Eleven

The cold took the breath out of him, and Charlie kicked hard, pulling John behind him. He swum towards what he hoped was the base of the cistern. But as he kicked, he lost all sense of direction and all he could see was darkness.

His fingers touched brickwork and he ranged his hands desperately over the solid wall. It was all the same. Flat narrow bricks. No change in shape. Nothing to indicate a way out. His lungs were starting to strain now.

Charlie felt for the string at his belt, where John's bulk pull the string taut.

That way is up, he thought, setting his inner compass by the string. *This way is down.*

He adjusted his search and now his fingertips hit an arch shape where the bricks formed a mouth.

An opening!

Grabbing John's wrist, Charlie swam for the gap without checking how large it was. He felt his back touch brick, his legs hit the stonework. Then he was through, pulling John behind.

They emerged in a wide body of water and Charlie's lungs had reached capacity. His legs slowed, starved of oxygen. He felt John flailing, panicking as his breath ran out.

There must be a way through.

Charlie kicked desperately but all was black. His mind swam. There was no air left. Nothing for his mind to fix on. Only the dark cold water all around.

Something was pulling his wrist. John was tugging at the string. Charlie followed the line of contact. And there it was. The faintest of yellow lights. It seemed to be coming closer. A candle flame?

Then he felt John lifted and wrenched away. And in another moment, strong arms lifted him free.

'God moves in mysterious ways,' said a good-natured voice. 'How came you to be swimming in the old sewer?'

Chapter Twelve

Charlie opened his eyes, spat water and righted himself. He swivelled in panic and then breathed out in relief to see John gasping with his back against the stone sewer wall.

He felt hands lift him to a sitting position. Then a kindly face met his.

The man's hair was cut in the style of a Roundhead soldier. He was dressed as a vicar, in a plain black overcoat with a square of white handkerchief at his neck and a black cap.

'I heard noises beneath my house,' the man explained. 'It connects to the old sewer and we use it sometimes. Did you come to flood the church?' he accused. 'You and your large friend?'

Charlie made the connection.

'So you're the bathhouse vicar,' he said.

The man blinked gently. He didn't seem surprised by the accusation.

'If you've come to make trouble,' he said, 'I'll give no names.'

Charlie shook his head.

'We didn't come to break up your church. I'm a thief-taker. Paid to find Nancy's stolen thimble.'

The cleric gave a sharp intake of breath.

'You're here to find poor Nancy's killer,' he said.

'I hunt stolen property,' corrected Charlie. 'I leave murders to the Watch.'

The vicar eyed him.

'Someone opened the sluice,' said Charlie, pointing to the water washing through the sewer. 'It wasn't us. Did you see anyone else down here? Or near the bathhouse?'

The vicar hesitated, then to Charlie's surprise he nodded.

'From my window I noticed someone near the bathhouse,' he said. 'A local lad. I didn't think anything of it. He comes to church sometimes and I assumed he wanted to say some prayers. I'm sure he would never …'

'Did this lad have red hair?' asked Charlie.

Dumbly, the vicar nodded.

'Where did he go?' asked Charlie, heaving himself up.

'I didn't see,' said the cleric. 'But you won't catch him. The boy is part-vagrant and adept at evading the justices.'

'He hasn't met me yet. Is there anything else you can tell us about the boy? Or Nancy's thimble?'

'You and your friend had best come with me,' decided the vicar. 'I've a fire you can dry yourselves by. I'll help you any way I can.'

'Do you know the Fitzgilberts?' asked Charlie, as he and John followed the vicar out of the sewer.

The man hesitated.

'No,' he said slowly. 'But I'll be meeting Elizabeth this evening.'

'You're ministering in her cell?' asked Charlie, confused. He'd imagined this would fall to Elizabeth's own vicar.

'I'm the only man of her faith who'd brave her witchcraft,' said the holy man with a faint smile. 'But I'm not ministering.' He eyed Charlie uneasily. 'You haven't heard,' he decided. 'Elizabeth had a fit, perhaps an hour ago. She was raving. Shouting things. They took it as evidence of witchcraft, and tried her in her cell.'

'They found her guilty?' asked Charlie, feeling ice settle in his stomach. He'd liked Elizabeth. For all her stubbornness, he admired her bravery.

'Guilty of witchcraft and murder,' said the vicar. 'I'm to read her last rites. She burns tomorrow.'

Chapter Thirteen

John and Charlie sat in the vicar's wooden house, steaming gently before the large fire. He had warmed them cups of wine with spices. His home was plain and comfortable, with a few simple chairs.

'Nancy fled to London,' the cleric was explaining, 'after some scandal in her hometown.'

'What scandal?' asked Charlie as he drank.

'We never asked. She told us she'd been wronged and we believed her.'

'You took a girl into your church, and never asked what scandal she escaped?'

'Forgiveness is at the heart of Christian living,' said the vicar. 'Nancy was eager to join our church. It was enough for us.'

'Did she travel from Lancashire alone?' asked Charlie.

'Nancy told me she came to London with her brother. But he was a feckless sort. In and out of debtors' prison. She did well to get into service, where her wages were her own.'

'Did you think Nancy a good girl?'

The vicar gave a small smile.

'I did. But she was unfortunate to be so lovely in her looks. Nancy attracted a great deal of interest she didn't want. Lord Gilbert took to visiting the Fitzgilberts' often, after she was employed.' The cleric raised his eyebrows to confirm the insinuation.

'You know Lord Gilbert?' asked Charlie.

'Know of him,' said the vicar. 'Like all of us in these parts. People say when he's not drinking he's fucking, though he must be near sixty now.'

'What of this red-headed boy,' said Charlie, 'he was in love with Nancy?'

'His name is Patrick. And yes, I think he likely was. He'd follow her around. I saw Nancy rebuff him a few times. Politely but firmly, as kind women do.'

'Did you think him the person who gave Nancy the silver thimble?' asked Charlie.

'Poor Patrick could not afford an expensive item like that.' The vicar's gentle features flickered uneasily. 'I was very concerned about the thimble. I even told Fitzgilbert. Though I'm not in the habit of telling tales,' he added. 'But with Lord Gilbert making visits … That man has more bastard children than legitimate ones. Only last year he ruined some poor local girl.'

'But you thought Nancy sensible,' confirmed Charlie.

'Women can be giddy when it comes to baubles. I hoped her sensible. But the evidence was she hadn't been.'

'What of Nancy's fortune-teller?'

'I didn't approve of course,' smiled the vicar. 'Some old crone telling stories.'

'Do you know where to find her?'

The cleric shook his head. 'Nancy assured me she only had a few tarot cards turned. I didn't object so long as she did no other occult divination.'

'Did Nancy come to you for exorcism?' asked Charlie.

The vicar looked slightly taken aback.

'Of course Nancy came for exorcism,' he said eventually. 'It's the main practice of our church. I assumed you knew.'

'Patrick too?' asked Charlie.

'Yes. I think it did him good for a time. Many troubled people come to me,' the vicar added. 'I've made it my life's work to relieve them.'

John and Charlie exchanged glances. This wasn't the usual practice of churches in London.

'Our exorcisms are Bible readings and blessings with holy water,' said the cleric carefully. 'Nancy submitted herself only once. I think she may have been expecting harsher treatment. Because of Fitzgilbert.'

He waited a moment, his eyes assessing Charlie.

'You didn't know Fitzgilbert carried out exorcisms?' he decided.

'Fitzgilbert performed exorcisms on Nancy?' said Charlie, shocked.

'Not on Nancy. On his poor wife.'

The vicar shook his head. He looked sad. 'I wanted to intervene. But Elizabeth is Fitzgilbert's property. Both legally and in the eyes of God.'

'Fitzgilbert was cruel then?'

'I can't tell you if his nature is cruel,' said the cleric. 'But his methods of expunging evil are.' He looked directly at Charlie.

'Elizabeth was denied food for days. She was purged, plunged in freezing water. Anything to weaken her spirit.'

Charlie swallowed, remembering the dignified woman in the prison cell.

'I don't agree with such methods,' continued the vicar. 'We use restraints to make the demons tremble. But we are gentle and never discomfort our subjects. I believe Fitzgilbert wanted to control his wife.'

The holy man's mouth twisted. 'There's a lot of talk in these parts,' he said slowly. 'I can't say how much is true. But it's said that Elizabeth wanted Nancy to leave the house.'

'Why?'

'Elizabeth thought Nancy cursed. Possessed by the Devil.'

Chapter Fourteen

'What now?' asked John, as they left the vicar's comfortable home.

'The fortune-teller,' said Charlie.

'We don't know where she is.'

'We do. The vicar told us Nancy had tarot cards read. That's a City trick. The fortune-tellers near Ald Gate are not so skilled. They divine from spit and feathers,' he added, thinking of the simple women who clustered around Ald Gate promising to foretell marriages and births.

'So the fortune-teller is in the City?' asked John, his forehead wrinkling.

'She *was* in the City,' corrected Charlie. 'She moved near the Ald Gate. In which case she'll be simple enough to spot. City fortune-tellers hang the sign of Merlin's head,' he added, in answer to John's uncertain expression. 'Bethnal Green folk hang a palm.'

'Right then,' said John, ready to go.

'You don't need to come along,' said Charlie. 'An old crone is hardly dangerous. But if you'd still wish to do me a service, you might seek out the silversmith in the Bucket of Blood. See if he's heard anything yet about a silver thimble being struck.'

John nodded and set off south. Charlie turned west, towards the band of women who plied their wares around Ald Gate.

The sign of Merlin's head swung amid the cluster of barbershop and fortune-teller palms. Charlie made a quick assessment.

This building, towards the back.

He slipped between a loaded dung cart and two beggar boys. A mouldering rug hung in place of a door, shedding a cloud of tiny flies as Charlie pushed it aside.

For a moment the dark room appeared empty. Then a shifting pile of rags moved and two rheumy eyes blinked forth. Charlie waited for his vision to adjust to the gloom. Old Joan was hunchbacked, her face folded in layers of brown skin. Shreds of threadbare fabric covered her ancient bulk and Charlie suspected her feet hadn't been seen in a long time.

'Don't often see menfolk,' she observed, in a creaking voice. 'Will you know of a girl?'

'In a manner of speaking,' said Charlie. 'I want to know of a girl who came to have her fortune told here. Nancy. A maidservant for the Fitzgilberts in Bethnal Green.'

'Many maidservants,' said Old Joan cagily. 'They're mostly who I see.'

Charlie brought forth a fistful of coins. The fortune-teller's eyes widened hungrily. Carefully, he placed a penny in her palm.

'I've four more,' he said, as her hand closed more quickly around the money than he would have thought her age capable of.

She beckoned for his hand. Slowly, he extended it.

The fortune-teller's strong fingers closed on his and she let out a hissing breath. Her eyes flicked up to his.

'You,' she said. 'You are destined for greatness. Descended from kings.'

Charlie shook his head.

'I don't want my fortune,' he said. 'I need to know about Nancy.'

She kept her tight grip on his hand. After a moment she seemed satisfied by what she saw in his palm.

'Nancy was in love,' she said, releasing her grip. 'Came to me for charms to break the spell.'

'She didn't want to be in love?'

The fortune-teller shook her head, looking at him craftily.

'Did she tell you who he was?' asked Charlie.

Old Joan held out her hand. Charlie dropped in another penny. The fingers closed. She sat back, watching him.

'Nancy never gave me a name,' she said finally. 'But it must have been that red-headed lad. He had something on Nancy. Lured her into alleyways, backstreets.'

'The red-headed boy was Nancy's secret lover?' asked Charlie, trying to fit the likelihood of this with what he knew.

'I couldn't say,' replied the fortune-teller. 'Only she was scared enough of him to do what she was told. She gave him money.'

Old Joan closed her mouth with deliberate finality. Charlie slid another penny into her grasp.

'Is that why Nancy kept the poppet and the shoe charm?' he asked. 'She was scared of this man?'

He drew out the corn dolly. The bearded man with the cross strapped to him.

The fortune-teller took it gently and turned it in her leathery hands.

'This is the green man,' she said. 'Jack of the fields.'

'Who is he?' Charlie had a vague recollection of the name. He was someone dangerous and unpredictable.

Old Joan laughed.

'The green man is life itself,' she cackled. 'A force of nature.' The yellowed whites of her eyes swivelled then lighted on Charlie's. 'He's in all of us,' she said. 'Some more than others. Nancy more than most. *You*,' she concluded, 'have a lot of him.'

'What does it mean?' asked Charlie, confused. 'Why would Nancy have this charm?'

'Is it not apparent? To a clever man as you?' The old woman sat back, pleased.

Charlie gave his third penny.

'Nancy,' said the fortune-teller, 'was scared of herself.'

She tapped the cross. 'I made this charm for her. To tame her wild ways.'

Old Joan eyed him, assessing. 'Nancy had dark things in her future,' she said. 'Dark and violent things. I gave her herbs. To keep her safe. To fortify her heart. But she lets him in. Nancy meets him in secret. And he will do a great violence to her. I've seen it.'

'Who?' pressed Charlie. 'Who does Nancy meet in secret?' This time his last penny was out ready for her.

'You know who,' nodded the fortune-teller, ignoring the penny and digging her fingers into Charlie's arm. 'Nancy meets with the Devil himself.'

Chapter Fifteen

Charlie was waiting thoughtfully outside the fortune-teller's when John lumbered into view. He was sweating with the exertion of coming from the silversmith's shop on Threadneedle Street.

'I learned a little,' said Charlie, as he neared. 'Though how much is true is hard to say.'

'I learned much,' replied John. 'Your silversmith has discovered who made the thimble.'

Charlie stood straighter.

'Who?'

'I can hardly believe it myself,' said John. 'The thimble was ordered by Mistress Fitzgilbert.'

Elizabeth Fitzgilbert made the thimble.

The revelation clarified a rush of half-formed suspicions. Facts began coming together in Charlie's mind. What had Fitzgilbert said of Nancy?

'She had no interest in men. Had none of that silliness ...'

Suddenly things fitted.

John was shaking his large head. 'I can't think what it could mean,' he said.

'I think I might,' replied Charlie, the conversation with the fortune-teller making better sense. 'I think Elizabeth Fitzgilbert and Nancy were lovers.'

John's mouth dropped in a wide gape.

'The mistress of the house and the maid?' he said.

'It's not the first time it's happened,' shrugged Charlie. 'Two women in close proximity. It would explain much – why Nancy believed Elizabeth possessed. Why she herself underwent exorcisms.'

John nodded slowly.

'Then you think Elizabeth Fitzgilbert is the killer?' he suggested.

'It's possible. But I think it unlikely. We need to find the red-headed boy.'

'How might we discover him?'

'City law decrees Nancy will be buried today,' said Charlie slowly. 'Most likely in the paupers' pit in Shoreditch.' He paused. 'I've a feeling our red-headed friend will be at the graveyard tonight.'

'What makes you think so?'

'Something the fortune-teller said.'

Chapter Sixteen

'A graveyard late at night.' John gave a shudder. 'There'll be spectres and all sorts come out soon. What makes you so sure he'll be here?'

They were hiding in the hedges at Shoreditch. John was naturally superstitious and it had taken an additional bribe of a meat pie to bring him along.

'The way Nancy is buried,' said Charlie, 'will draw him out. If he is who I think he is.'

'What's wrong with the way she's buried?' John was peering into the moonlit graveyard. A huge dark pit yawned out at them. They could just make out the shapes of dead limbs and the white residue of quicklime.

'He won't like it,' said Charlie.

John gave another theatrical shudder and crossed himself. He opened his mouth to speak again, when they heard a sound across the graveyard.

Charlie raised a warning finger. They both craned further forward to look. A shape in the dark was making its way to the graveside. They watched as the shadowy figure hopped into the grave. Moments later a candle flame bloomed from deep in the pit.

'This way,' hissed Charlie. 'Stay close.'

John nodded and skulked behind as Charlie made his way to the graveside. At the edge Charlie peered over. Dead faces leered up, unseeing gummy eyes staring. The candle flame burned. Something was wrong.

Charlie leaped aside just as hands grabbed at his long leather coat. He dodged, and someone lunged at him again. Charlie swerved, took hold of his assailant and they both plunged headlong into the corpse-filled pit.

John was reaching for his crucifix as Charlie rolled and tussled.

'It's not a ghost,' gasped Charlie, grabbing a handful of quicklime and throwing it. His assailant choked and cursed. Charlie took hold of him and pinned him to the cold stiff bodies.

The red-headed boy twisted and swore.

'There's no need to fight me,' said Charlie, wrestling to retain control. 'We want the same as you. To find Nancy's killer.'

The boy's struggle eased slightly.

'Then why do you visit the witch in prison?' demanded a surprisingly youthful voice.

'To discover what she knows,' replied Charlie. He let go, sensing restraint was no longer necessary. The red-haired boy groped for his candle and lifted it. For an instant Charlie thought he would attack again. But instead he offered a hand.

'I'm Patrick,' he said.

'I know who you are,' said Charlie. 'You're Nancy's brother.'

Chapter Seventeen

'When the vicar said Nancy came to London with her brother,' explained Charlie, 'I suspected it was you. He thought you in love with Nancy. He saw her rebuff your advances in church.'

Patrick wiped his nose.

'You knew I'd be here?' he said.

'A brother doesn't like his sister buried in a paupers' grave,' said Charlie. 'I guessed you'd come to take her remains somewhere better.'

'But how did you know who I was?'

'Nancy's fortune-teller. Who else could persuade her to meet in dangerous back alleys and give money? She wasn't a foolish girl.'

'No,' said Patrick. His face flushed suddenly and his eyes filled with tears. 'She was a good girl,' he said. 'A very good girl. Until that old hag …' He gritted his teeth. 'She corrupted her. Mistress Fitzgilbert.' He spat the words.

'They were lovers?' said Charlie.

Patrick nodded.

'And you think Elizabeth murdered Nancy?'

'Of course she did,' said Patrick miserably. 'Nancy was trying to do right. To stay Godly. She had exorcisms, to drive out the Devil. At first it wasn't enough. Her mistress's power was too strong. Then Nancy tried to leave that cursed house. And the witch killed her.'

'Nancy was going to leave the Fitzgilberts'?' said Charlie. 'I heard it the other way. That the mistress wanted free of the maid.'

'Nancy told me she was leaving.' Patrick gave a great sniff. 'She was an innocent. Then she came here under that old crow.'

'Yet Nancy left some scandal,' said Charlie, 'in her hometown.'

Patrick coloured and Charlie knew he'd guessed right. Nancy had other women lovers before Elizabeth Fitzgilbert.

'Might she have taken a man for a lover?' asked Charlie. 'Lord Gilbert? Or Mr Fitzgilbert?'

Patrick shook his head.

'She wasn't … that way suited,' he said. 'She hoped to change it. Through prayer. I daresay she would have married in the end. Perhaps unhappily.' His face contorted in ugly distaste. 'Elizabeth Fitzgilbert murdered my sister. I'm sure of it.'

'Then she must have the silver thimble?'

Patrick hesitated.

'What does the thimble have to do with it?'

'Her master thinks Nancy had the thimble the night she died,' said Charlie. 'It was missing from her body.'

Patrick's face appeared to be working through several thoughts at once.

'It isn't possible,' he managed.

'Why not?'

'Because I've seen the silver thimble,' said Patrick. 'And the man who has it couldn't have killed Nancy.'

'Who has the thimble?' It took every ounce of self-control for Charlie to keep his voice level.

'It was in his hanging pocket,' Patrick muttered. 'When I followed you to the bathhouse. I saw him take it out.'

'Who?' asked Charlie, though he'd formed a good guess.

'Nancy's vicar,' said Patrick. 'He has the thimble.'

'You're sure?'

'I … I believe so.' Patrick looked flustered. 'I saw it only for an instant. I assumed Nancy had given it to him to help cleanse her soul. It was from her,' he spat. 'The witch woman.'

Charlie looked at John.

'The vicar will be with Mistress Fitzgilbert on the death cart tomorrow,' he said. 'If the thimble is where Patrick says, he will have it with him.'

Chapter Eighteen

'You think the vicar is the killer?' asked John, as morning sunlight spilled across the Thames. Clink prisoners were carted over the river at dawn and they could hear the rumbling prison cart rolling closer.

'It's possible,' said Charlie, who had learned not to prejudge a kind face. 'If he has the thimble he certainly has some explaining to do.'

'And if it isn't the vicar?'

'Then it's most likely Elizabeth Fitzgilbert,' said Charlie. 'She's always had the best motive. I've got a few questions for her too,' he added.

'How long will the cart stop at Newgate?'

'Long enough,' said Charlie. It wasn't the first time he'd questioned a condemned prisoner on their way to Tyburn Hill. 'Men and women to be executed are slow to load,' he added.

The cart rounded the corner. A jumble of ragged people were clustered on top. There were two armed guards and a customary black and white clad holy man at the head of the cart. It was the bathhouse vicar.

He recognised Charlie and smiled encouragingly. Then he broke from the cart and came closer.

'You are here to give comfort?' he asked. 'She needs it.'

'How is she?' asked Charlie, his eyes roving the cart for Elizabeth. He caught sight of her, pale and hunched, sat with three other stunned-looking women.

'Doesn't yet believe her fate. You wish to speak with her?'

Charlie nodded.

'She's in a low state of mind,' said the vicar. 'I think she believed God would intervene. Go to her. I'll be sure the guards don't trouble you.'

Charlie clapped him firmly on the shoulder in thanks. As he did, he slid a light pickpocket's hand inside the holy man's coat.

'Will you watch the pyre?' asked Charlie.

The vicar's eyes widened in shock and Charlie quickly untied his hanging pocket.

'I'll be there with her,' he muttered, 'but I don't mean to watch.'

'Better that way,' agreed Charlie, tugging the pocket free. He stepped back, passing it to John. Then he moved towards the cart.

The wagon was loaded with poor skin-and-bone wretches. Elizabeth was standing now, working a Bible in her hands. She gave a gasp when she saw Charlie.

'Elizabeth,' he said.

She made the ghost of a smile and moved forward.

'Come to set me free?' she asked. Charlie's heart shrank at the tinge of hope in her voice.

'No,' he said regretfully.

She moved to the edge of the cart, out of hearing of the other prisoners.

'You wouldn't be here,' she said, 'if you understood the evil I'm capable of.'

'You and Nancy were lovers,' said Charlie. 'I know it.'

Elizabeth's hands trembled.

'The vicar said that you thought Nancy possessed by the Devil.'

She nodded.

'I do believe that,' she said. 'We both were. If we were not …' Unexpectedly, her face reddened and tears sprang to her eyes. 'If I were not,' Elizabeth whispered, 'how could she have made me feel … what I felt?'

'You loved her,' Charlie said simply.

Elizabeth wiped the falling tears away. Her hands reached for the string tied round her neck. She saw Charlie's gaze follow her hands and drew them away quickly.

He thought he caught the edge of what the string held, tucked beneath her dress. It was a flash of silver.

'And sometimes hated her too,' she said haltingly. 'Though we knew it to be wrong, Nancy was the greatest happiness I ever knew on this earth. But we knew, we both knew, it was the Devil …' She stopped and took a shuddering breath. 'He made us do those terrible things. But I loved her. God forgive me.'

'Perhaps it isn't too late,' suggested Charlie. 'If I can find the silver thimble it might help me find the killer. Nancy's brother told me the vicar had it.'

'Nancy's brother?'

'The red-haired apprentice.'

Understanding dawned in Elizabeth's face. 'That makes sense,' she muttered. 'The boy is her brother.' Her green eyes lifted to

Charlie's. 'But how would her vicar have the thimble? Such a thing isn't possible.'

Guards were shoving extra prisoners onto the cart now. Elizabeth was jostled out of view. She pushed back to the front.

'If the vicar was Nancy's killer,' reasoned Charlie, 'he might have taken it from her body.'

'No.' Elizabeth was shaking her head. Her hand reached again for the cord around her neck. 'It isn't possible,' she said with surety. 'Nancy's brother was mistaken.'

'What makes you so sure?' asked Charlie.

'Because I …' More prisoners pushed her aside. This time she was hemmed in tight on all sides. Her face set itself in piety.

'I leave my fate to God,' she shouted over the noise. 'When Nancy died I resolved to meddle no more in earthly affairs.'

Charlie realised immediately.

She won't tell me like this. Not shouted from a prison cart.

'You must have some thoughts as to who murdered her,' he urged. 'Her killer came from inside the house. They used a candlestick or something like it. You can't easily hide such a large weapon. The person would have been known to you.'

Elizabeth's eyes filled with tears.

'At least confess,' said Charlie. 'Say you were her lover. They'll hang you instead of a burning.'

She shook her head.

'I won't own to something I'm innocent of,' she said loudly. 'I trust in God. If he believes me innocent I'll be saved.' She looked uncertain suddenly. 'If my love for Nancy was evil,' she concluded, 'then I must burn.'

'God won't save you,' said Charlie. 'Please. You've never seen a burning.'

But before he could say more, the cart lurched and guards pushed him roughly back.

Charlie backed away as Elizabeth was hidden among the new crowd of prisoners. John stepped to his side.

'Is she guilty?'

'If she is,' said Charlie, 'she's a good liar.'

John pulled out the vicar's hanging pocket.

'Shall we find out?' he asked.

He let the pocket fall open. Their faces dropped in disappointment.

'It's not here,' said John, eyeing the meagre contents of the pocket. There were a few coins and a plain silver ring.

Charlie picked one out.

'Patrick mistook,' he said, disappointment flooding him. He'd pinned his last hopes on some evidence in the vicar's pocket. 'It could resemble a thimble from a distance,' he added, dropping it back in the purse.

'How could you mistake a ring for a thimble?' protested John.

'His sister had just been brutally killed,' said Charlie. 'Patrick believes a witch killed her. A witch who gave Nancy a betrothal thimble. He's probably seeing silver thimbles everywhere.'

Charlie watched the cart lumbering slowly away. He called to the guard bringing up the rear.

'Give this to the vicar!' he called, tossing the pocket. 'It fell from his coat. He should take better care in future.'

The guard caught the pocket and nodded, looking confused.

'We wasted time,' Charlie concluded sadly, 'on a wild goose chase. If Elizabeth is innocent it's too late to save her now.'

Chapter Nineteen

'Not going to watsh the witch-burning then?' slurred the silversmith, already drunk.

'No.' Charlie was on his third tankard of ale. He'd hoped it would help him think, but it was having the opposite effect. Images of Elizabeth burning were running through his mind.

He took another swig. A clutch of stray puppies were racing around the tavern floor, growling and worrying furniture. The landlord was half-heartedly shooing them out.

John clapped Charlie on the back, jolting him free of his thoughts.

'Don't take it hard,' said John. 'There had to be one stolen thing you didn't find. You'd end up accused of witchcraft yourself if it wasn't so.'

Charlie managed a small smile.

'I'll find the thimble,' he said.

'Perhaps the wife did it after all,' suggested John.

'Looks that way.' Charlie was playing the image of Elizabeth over in his head. Straight-backed and sober. She wasn't a soft woman. But was she capable of murder? He tried to picture her wielding a weapon. Smashing it into her lover's face. It still didn't fit.

The murder weapon. It had always troubled Charlie.

A candlestick? What else could have done that damage?

He replayed the scene in his mind.

The window was open. Fitzgilbert claimed Nancy never opened the window.

The silversmith raised his tankard and took a deep draft. It clanked against the various wares strung around his neck. 'Pass me the barrel so I might take the dregs,' he said to Charlie. 'Waste not, want not.'

Suddenly Charlie realised what had been bothering him about the missing thimble. And he knew where to find it.

He turned to John. 'How long until your fight?'

'Long time,' replied John. 'Not till sunset. Perhaps later.'

'We need to get to Tyburn,' said Charlie. 'To save an innocent woman.'

Chapter Twenty

Elizabeth Fitzgilbert stood tall on the pyre. Her eyes ranged the jeering crowd. Women were crossing themselves, holding up their children for a better look. The odd missile still flew her way, but mostly they'd been used up on the bumping cart.

She was grateful the bonfire was of a modest size. A neat fan of branches lifted her barely a foot off the ground and allowed her husband to stand almost by her side.

Fitzgilbert was a few feet from his wife, staring out into the crowd. His ratty features were frozen in shock, as though he expected at any moment to wake from a dream.

At the edge of the crowd she could see Lord Gilbert. His contemptuous expression was softened by drink. A goblin-faced prostitute hung off his arm, a barrel of wine tucked securely beneath her skirts. Lord Gilbert felt obliged to show disgust for his daughter-in-law's crime by attending. But he'd brought the tavern with him.

'Burn the witch!' shrieked a woman with a face full of boils. 'Burn them all!'

There was a murmur of agreement.

Elizabeth watched as the last convict was led to the scaffold. Nineteen bodies already hung limp. The women had gone first, out of compassion. But the pyre was being left until last. The executioner had a sense of theatre. He knew the people had come to see the witch burn. Bets had been made whether she'd survive the flames and fly to freedom.

Elizabeth looked up at the sky. It was a sunny day. A few clouds scudding across the heavens. In a sudden certainty, she knew what awaited her.

She watched as the noose was tightened about the criminal's neck. The vicar stepped forward on the scaffold, his face earnest, and put a comforting hand on the condemned man's arm.

'Elizabeth.' She turned distractedly. Her husband was looking at her devotedly. 'I'm sorry,' said Fitzgilbert. 'For what I did.'

Elizabeth managed a half-smile.

'It was arrogant,' he said. 'And cruel.'

His fingers twitched, but he restrained himself from pulling free the snuff box. His eyes drifted to Lord Gilbert, who was holding out his wine tankard for his half-dressed companion to refill.

'I told myself I did it for your good.' Fitzgilbert hung his head, shamefaced. 'I know now,' he said, 'it was my own guilt and shame I tried to exorcise.'

Elizabeth slid out a cool hand. It closed on her husband's.

'You wronged me,' she said. 'But I forgive you.'

They were interrupted by the loud sound of the trapdoor opening. The mob shrieked and cheered as the convict swung.

Fitzgilbert stepped towards his wife. He brought forth a small bag of gunpowder, which he tied gently around her neck.

'When the flames get high,' he said, 'it will be over quickly.'

'It shouldn't be allowed!' shrieked a woman from the crowd. 'Witches of good families should not be spared the full burning!'

Fitzgilbert kissed his wife and drew back, tears in his eyes.

The executioner began making his way to the pyre.

Chapter Twenty-One

'I know where the thimble is,' said Charlie as they raced west from Covent Garden.

'Where?' John's face was red with the exertion of running.

'It was right in front of us,' said Charlie, weaving through the crowded roads. 'The murder weapon too. And if I'm right, both will be at Tyburn with her.'

'It's already afternoon,' panted John. 'It's a mile and a half away. Mistress Elizabeth will be aflame.'

'We have to try.' Charlie assessed the streets. 'We'll cut through Marylebone village,' he decided. 'Less crowds. From there it's only half a mile on dirt tracks.'

John began to tire as they reached Marylebone. Charlie settled into a steady jog. On the outskirts of Tyburn they both realised it was hopeless.

The crowds were massed so thickly round execution hill it would take an hour to wade through. And high on the hill they could see twenty bodies already dangling on nooses.

'Come on,' said Charlie, not willing to give up. 'We can't see the pyre. It hasn't been lit.'

'We'll never make it,' said John.

'We have to. Elizabeth Fitzgilbert is innocent. I'll not have her death on my conscience.'

'Why doesn't she protest her innocence?' gasped John. 'She let us think she was guilty.'

'Because she thinks she has sinned against God. And will only believe she's forgiven if he saves her.'

'Maybe he will.'

'It's not been his way so far,' said Charlie, shoving through the crowd.

He pushed past a burly fish wife.

'I've waited since noon!' she shrieked. 'You'll not cheat me of my view!' She lunged unsuccessfully at Charlie's coat. Others in the crowd began to turn and shout now, as Charlie and John bludgeoned their way through. People formed ranks, barring their path.

Then a mighty cheer went up.

Charlie felt his stomach drop.

'They've lit the pyre,' he said grimly.

A winding line of smoke drifted up on the horizon. Charlie felt his blood turn to ice. They were too late. Elizabeth was aflame.

He looked at the bank of people crammed in ahead of them. At the smoke in the distance. There was no way they could save her.

Horror coiled in Charlie. Any moment now, they'd hear her screams.

Something splashed against his arm. Then again. Charlie looked down distractedly.

'I don't believe it.' He turned to John. 'Rain.'

Chapter Twenty-Two

Confusion rippled through the crowd. Spatters of rain were falling faster now. Some of the bystanders began to break away, covering their heads, heading for shelter. As the crowd thinned, a pathway opened up. Charlie and John made for the smoking pyre.

''Tis God's doing,' Charlie heard a woman say.

'That or witchcraft,' said a man. 'But the executioner will get that pyre burning. Rain or no rain.'

Yet the rain will slow him down, thought Charlie.

They made their way through the people, some of whom were scattering in all directions. Others were taking advantage of the weather to occupy a better spot near the front.

John and Charlie shouldered forward until a tall mound of wood came into view. The people were crammed in tighter here. Die-hard execution-goers.

Charlie made out Elizabeth's tall body, strapped to the central post. The executioner was at the base of it with a bellows, reigniting the smouldering flames.

Charlie reached the pyre, pushing aside a scrawny man and his enormous wife. Elizabeth met his eye and her face flowered in hope.

The rain seemed to be easing. People in the crowd began shouting for Charlie to get back from the pyre. The executioner stood with his bellows still in hand. He made towards Charlie, ready to push him back.

'Elizabeth Fitzgilbert is innocent!' shouted Charlie. The executioner hesitated. A few bystanders murmured uncertainly.

'But the murderer is here today!' added Charlie, taking a gamble that the drama of an accusation would work.

Several eyes swung to Fitzgilbert at his wife's side. His mouth worked comically. A few other women were glaring at Lord Gilbert. His prostitute took a considered step backwards. He lowered the tankard and his hand moved to the heavy sword at his hip, drink-dulled eyes wary.

The executioner stood, temporarily forgetting his role to fan the flames. The fire sizzled and began to die beneath the rain.

'There was a fair trial,' he said. 'You've nothing to prove what you say.'

'I have the thimble,' said Charlie, 'stolen from the dead girl's body. And the weapon used to cave in her skull.'

A thrill went through the remaining crowd. This was worth hearing.

'Show me,' demanded the executioner.

'They're both here in front of us,' said Charlie. 'The killer holds the murder weapon in his hands. But the thimble is no longer a thimble. It was cut to make a ring.'

Elizabeth's mouth was moving in prayer.

'Puritans give silver thimbles for engagements,' continued Charlie. 'I couldn't understand how they could justify it. With a ring for the ceremony as well. Then I realised. The thimble doesn't stay a thimble. It becomes the wedding band.'

He paused.

'On the wedding day they slice off the top,' he concluded, 'and make it a ring.' He gave a small smile. 'Waste not, want not.'

Charlie pointed.

'Her killer,' he continued, 'was in love with her. He had Nancy's ring in his hanging pocket. But he couldn't resist wearing it for Elizabeth's execution.'

Charlie stepped towards the vicar.

'He has the ring,' said Charlie. 'On his wedding finger. And he carries the sacrament. The heavy cross used to murder Nancy.'

Chapter Twenty-Three

'It's a lie!' The vicar's face was an angry mask.

The executioner was moving towards him.

'See the bevelled edge,' said Charlie, as he pulled the ring roughly from the holy man's finger. 'The uneven top. It's been cut.'

The vicar gave a high-pitched laugh. He held the sacrament closer to his body.

'How could I do such a thing?' he said.

'You fell in love with Nancy,' said Charlie. 'She confided in you her relationship with Mistress Fitzgilbert and you convinced her she was possessed by the Devil. You went to the Fitzgilberts' house to perform an exorcism on Nancy. You threw open the window,' continued Charlie, 'to let out the demon. And you had with you the murder weapon. The sacrament. A large cross, heavy like a candlestick. You would have found it easy to conceal the weapon.'

The vicar had paled.

'It's not true,' he said. 'Every holy man has a sacrament. And this is a silver ring, no more. Without the top no one can say ...'

Charlie opened his mouth then shut it again. He flicked a glance at Elizabeth.

It's up to you now, he thought, *I'll not tell if you don't want it.*

There was a pause. Then she spoke.

'I have the top,' said Elizabeth. 'It's around my neck.'

A shocked murmur rippled through the crowd.

Elizabeth nodded to her husband. He untied the pouch of gunpowder from around her neck. Then he drew up the cord from beneath her dress. Attached was a domed silver medallion with the studded cross.

Fitzgilbert tugged it free and handed it to the executioner, who fitted it to the top of the ring. He held it up to the crowd triumphantly. Shouts rang out.

'And how comes she by such a thing?' accused the vicar loudly. 'How does Elizabeth Fitzgilbert, a married lady, have part of a wedding ring for another woman?'

'It's no one's concern,' interjected Charlie, 'if two women exchange tokens of affection. Girls are fond of such practices.'

A few women in the crowd were nodding. One lifted a lock of hair tied at her neck and kissed it. The tide had turned firmly in Elizabeth's favour.

'But you,' Charlie pointed at the vicar, 'killed an innocent woman.'

The cleric pursed his lips. His face reddened.

'I never went to murder her,' he whispered. 'It was never my intention. I went to save her soul.'

'But you couldn't?' guessed Charlie. 'You couldn't make Nancy stop loving her mistress?'

'She was saying disgusting things,' spluttered the vicar. 'Things about Elizabeth. It was the Devil. He was speaking through Nancy. And I had to make her quiet. I had to …' He squeezed his eyes tight shut. 'I struck at the demon,' he said. 'But it was Nancy who fell.'

'You didn't just want to quieten a demon,' said Charlie. 'You wanted to black out Nancy's beautiful face. You were so ashamed she'd tempted you. And you were angry that your exorcism had failed.'

'She was a demon taunting me,' said the holy man. His voice was tight with rage. 'I can hardly say what happened. I just … I just kept hitting her.'

His eyes slipped across to Elizabeth.

'Mistress Fitzgilbert,' he pleaded. 'You must tell them. It was for Nancy's own good. The Devil was in her. You know that.'

He gestured to the crowd.

'Tell them,' he said, 'that the Devil possessed you both. But now he has been driven out and you commit yourself to God.'

Elizabeth was staring at him, grief burning in her green eyes.

'I can save you,' nodded the vicar. 'From your unnatural desires.'

Elizabeth's lips parted. She stood a little straighter.

'Untie me,' she said quietly. The executioner came towards her and cut free her hands. Elizabeth stepped from the pyre.

Then she turned and addressed herself to the crowd.

'My maid Nancy,' she announced, 'was the best sort of girl. With a blameless love for her friends. And this man,' Elizabeth raised a hand to point, 'murdered my Nancy. Whom we all loved.' Her voice faltered and she drew a gasping breath. In the crowd women were wiping away tears.

'I implore the justices,' concluded Elizabeth, 'to hang him for his crime.'

The request was caught up in a whisper. Then it raised to a chant. And soon the assembled mob were baying for the vicar's sentence.

'String him up!' shrieked a balding laundry woman.

The prison guard stepped forward and clapped a burly hand on the vicar's shoulder.

Elizabeth turned to her husband. Fitzgilbert stepped forward clumsily and embraced his wife.

She extricated herself after a moment and turned to Charlie.

'You came to prove my innocence,' she smiled. 'You're a better man than you pretend.'

'I came for the silver thimble,' he said, 'and my fee.'

Elizabeth took a step closer to him.

'Do you still believe God doesn't like London?' she asked.

'We're not in London,' Charlie pointed out with a grin. 'Tyburn is outside the City. But I've a new manner of understanding miracles,' he added. 'And if I'm ever in need of one, I'll come to you.'

A word from CS Quinn

I really hope you enjoyed reading this book as much as I enjoyed writing it. This was a short prelude to The Thief Taker series, which you can find on Amazon.

Would you like a **free secret scene** available only to my super readers?

Visit **www.thethieftaker.com/secretscene** to receive a chapter from Charlie's mysterious past. You'll also get access to historic images, London maps and people who inspired The Thief Taker series.